ZEBRAFISH

D0108115

57 UNIVERSITY

Peter H. Reynolds and FableVision present

ZEBRAFISH

Written by Sharon Emerson
Drawn by Renée Kurilla

Atheneum Books for Young Readers
New York • London • Toronto • Sydney • New Delhi

ATHENEUM BOOKS FOR YOUNG READERS
An imprint of Simon & Schuster Children's Publishing Division
1230 Avenue of the Americas, New York, New York 10020
This book is a work of fiction. Any references to historical events, real people, or real locales are used fictitiously. Other names, characters, places, and incidents are products of the author's imagination, and any resemblance to actual events or locales or persons, living or dead, is entirely coincidental.
Copyright © 2010 by Children's Hospital Boston
Photograph of zebrafish in p. 80 copyright © 2010 by Richard White
All rights reserved, including the right of reproduction in whole or in part in any form.
ATHENEUM BOOKS FOR YOUNG READERS is a registered trademark of Simon & Schuster, Inc.
For information about special discounts for bulk purchases, please contact Simon & Schuster Special Sales at 1-866-506-1949 or business@simonandschuster.com.
The Simon & Schuster Speakers Bureau can bring authors to your live event. For more information or to book an event, contact the Simon & Schuster Speakers Bureau at 1-866-248-3049 or visit our website at www.simonspeakers.com.
Also available in an Atheneum Books for Young Readers hardcover edition

FableVision

Book design by FableVision, Inc.
The text for this book is set in AGaramondPro, ArialMT, Slappy, Times New Roman, space-cowboy.
The illustrations for this book are inked and colored digitally.
Manufactured in China
0412 WGL
First Atheneum Books for Young Readers paperback edition June 2012
2 4 6 8 10 9 7 5 3 1
The Library of Congress has cataloged the hardcover edition as follows:
Emerson, Sharon.
Peter H. Reynolds and FableVision present Zebrafish / written by Sharon Emerson ; illustrated by Renée Kurilla. — 1st ed.
p. cm.
Title: Zebrafish
Summary: When their rock band becomes popular, five middle schoolers use their new fame to generate awareness (and donations) for an important cause.
ISBN 978-1-4169-9525-8 (hc)
1. Graphic novels. [1. Graphic novels. 2. Rock groups — Fiction. 3. Charities — Fiction.] I. Reynolds, Peter, 1961- II. Kurilla, Renee, ill. III. FableVision Studios. IV. Title.
PZ7.7.E47Pe 2010
741.5'973 — dc22 2009041683
ISBN 978-1-4169-9707-8 (pbk)
ISBN 978-1-4424-0609-4 (eBook)

Contents

1. Family 1
2. Induction 21
3. Cause and Effect 29
4. A Star Is Bored 32
5. What's in a Name? 39
6. Reentry 42
7. Upstaged 47
8. Take Two 53
9. Crushed 57
10. One Song 66
11. Intensification 68
12. Impact 72
13. Intervention 82
14. Reflection 84
15. Jam Session 91
16. Make It Better 94
17. Preshow 100
18. Zebrafish Effect 104
19. Encore 118

Afterword by Peter H. Reynolds 120

Thank you

For the inspiration:

Dr. Dario Fauza
Dr. Richard White

For the challenge:

Gary Goldberger
Kate Cotter
Shelley Brown
Janet Cady
Caitlyn Dlouhy
Dan Potash

For the help:

Bob Flynn
Didi Mitova
Samantha Wilder Oliver
Keith Zulawnik

1. Family

Late June...

Jay! Got my ax?
Right here, man.
Let's start the show!
260
ALLIE! Spotlight!
Eve of destruction, tax deduction, city inspectors, bill collectors—
HA! HA!

HA! *huff*
HA! HA!
Jay! You're missing notes!
Let me hear ya.
Let me hear ya.
Let me hear ya—
BOOOOOOOOOOOOOOOOOO!
Jay, are you coming to dinner with us?
Yes, Mrs. Plinko! Ha, ha! Thanks!
BOOOOO!

At Nearby University Chapel...

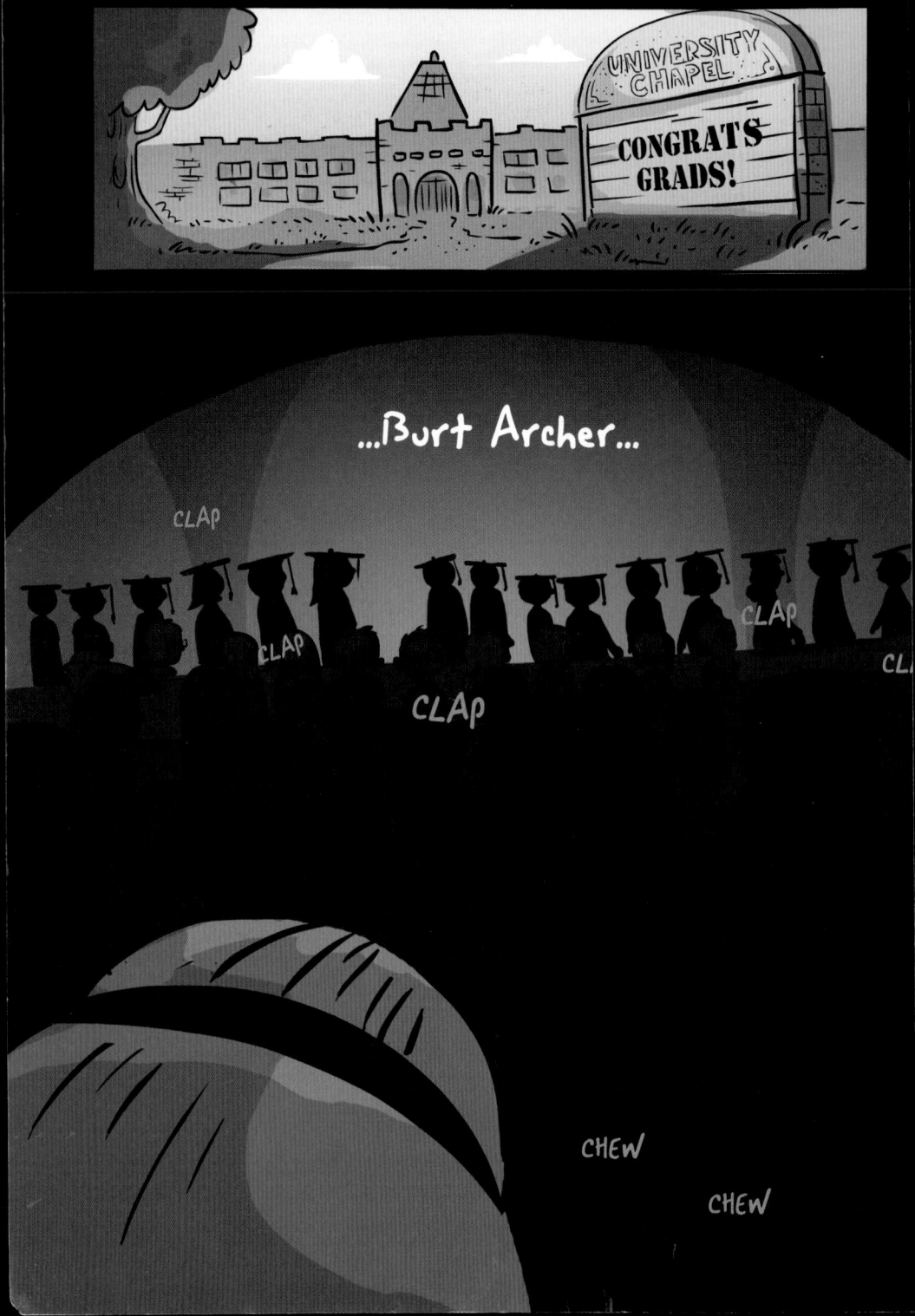

CLAP
CLAP
CLAP
CLAP
CLAP
...Ellen Cisco...
...Lucy Coho...
...Joe Dorado...
...Pablo Escolar...

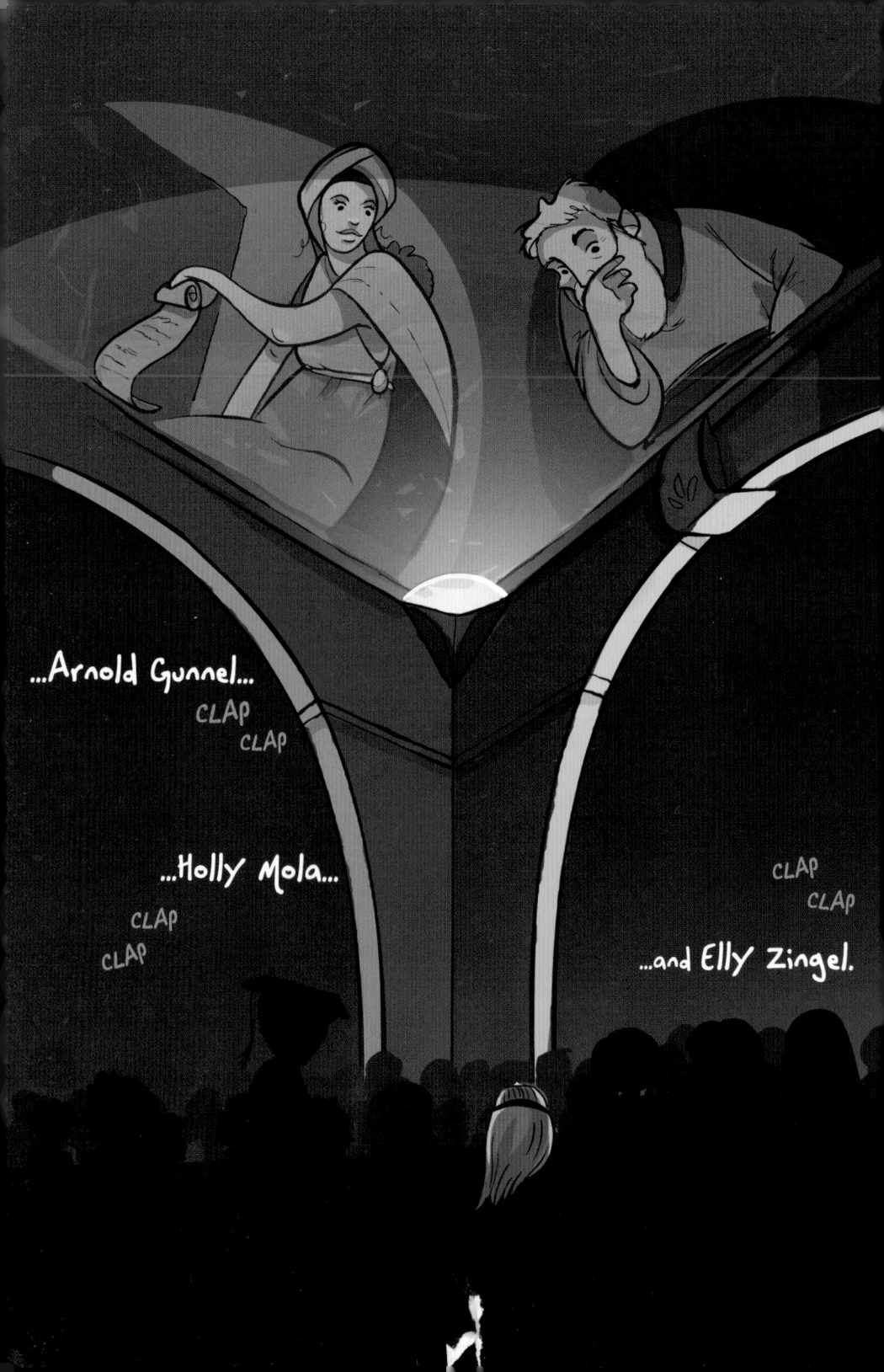
...Arnold Gunnel...
CLAP
CLAP
...Holly Mola...
CLAP
CLAP
CLAP
CLAP
...and Elly Zingel.

They said your name ages ago!
Hey, I sat through your graduation.
Yeah, but we had musical numbers.
Doesn't that look like Mom?
Who, Aristotle?
Which one is she?
He was one of the greatest thinkers of all time. He was a philosopher, poet, physicist, biologist...Sort of a Swiss Army scientist.
Can we go to Fudgie's now?

Later...
Fudgie's
Want to grab some free-range fries?

No time. Mom's on her way. Besides, I'm not even hungry...

...my stomach hurts.

I'll have the double fudgie burger with ja-la-pen-yo.
And for the young lady?
KID COMBOS
FUDGIE'S
KID COMBOS!
FUDGIE'S
I WANT! A FUDGIE DOG! PLEASE!

Kid combos are on the back.
I'll have the adult macaroni and cheese and an adult Coke.
There's only one kind of Coke.
Can I get that in a glass?
FUDGIE'S
KID COMBOS
FUDGIE'S

I wish we had a dog.
Dogs need a lot of attention. *text* *text*
But they also give a lot of attention.
You need attention?
That's what Mrs. Loach said.
Who?
The lady I used to talk to from my old school.
Oh, the social worker. *text* *text*
She said that the move would deepen my sense of detachment.
Did she have anything positive to say?

Yeah! Get a dog!
I don't think our building allows them.
How about Pepper?
Here you go.
Right next door? That's almost like having a dog!
NO! Pepper! Mrs. James's dog! Next door?!

The Next Day...

But...I s'pose he could use some fresh air. Let me get his leash.

Hold his leash tight!
And don't walk too fast!
125
Pepper's an old man!

WAIT!
PEPPER!
NOOOOOO!

Don't! Eat! Trash!

125
Hey!
Get that dog on a leash!

Later, Upstairs...

The Next Day...

wiggle
wiggle

Let's hope he doesn't get any bigger.
DO-IT-YOURSELF DOGGIE DOOR

2. Induction
Late August...
Hands off my Honey Puffs!
Vita...what's in your hair?
CRUNCH CRUNCH
Bolt of Blue.
CRUNCH
CHIMP
CRUNCH CRUNCH CRUNCH
It's your first day at school. Why would you do that?
I want to make a good impression.

Sheesh. Even Cleopatra dyed her hair when she was a teenager!
Cleopatra was bald. She shaved her head and wore wigs!
Really? How much is a wig?
Oh, no. Let's rewind. The blue is grea—
Is that my bus? That's my bus!
See ya later!
At the new lab!
Fourth floor! I remember!
Four-teenth! Four-TEENTH!

Southside School...

...OOOOOOOOOOOOOOOOOOOOOT
WHAT? Who?
I wasn't running!
Hey!
You, uh, left it really clean.
You got my old locker!
I'm Vita.
I'm J—
Jay!
Can you take this?

What? Why? Just put it in your locker!
It doesn't fit! I have twice as many books this year!
Why'd you even bring this to school?
I don't want Allie touching it. It's still new!
BRRIIIINNNNNNG!
Dude, it stops being new after five months.
Oh, great. Now I've got to drag it to class!

After School...

The New Lab...

Hey, Vita. Pull up a chair. I'm almost done.
It looks just like the old lab. But with a refrigerator!
It's empty.
But I'm thirsty.
There's a fountain down the hall.

Outside...
What'd you do for three hours?
Sketched. Was it bad?
Not like the biopsy.
Three more this month. Then they spread them out.
You've got another spinal tap next week?!

2. Cause and Effect

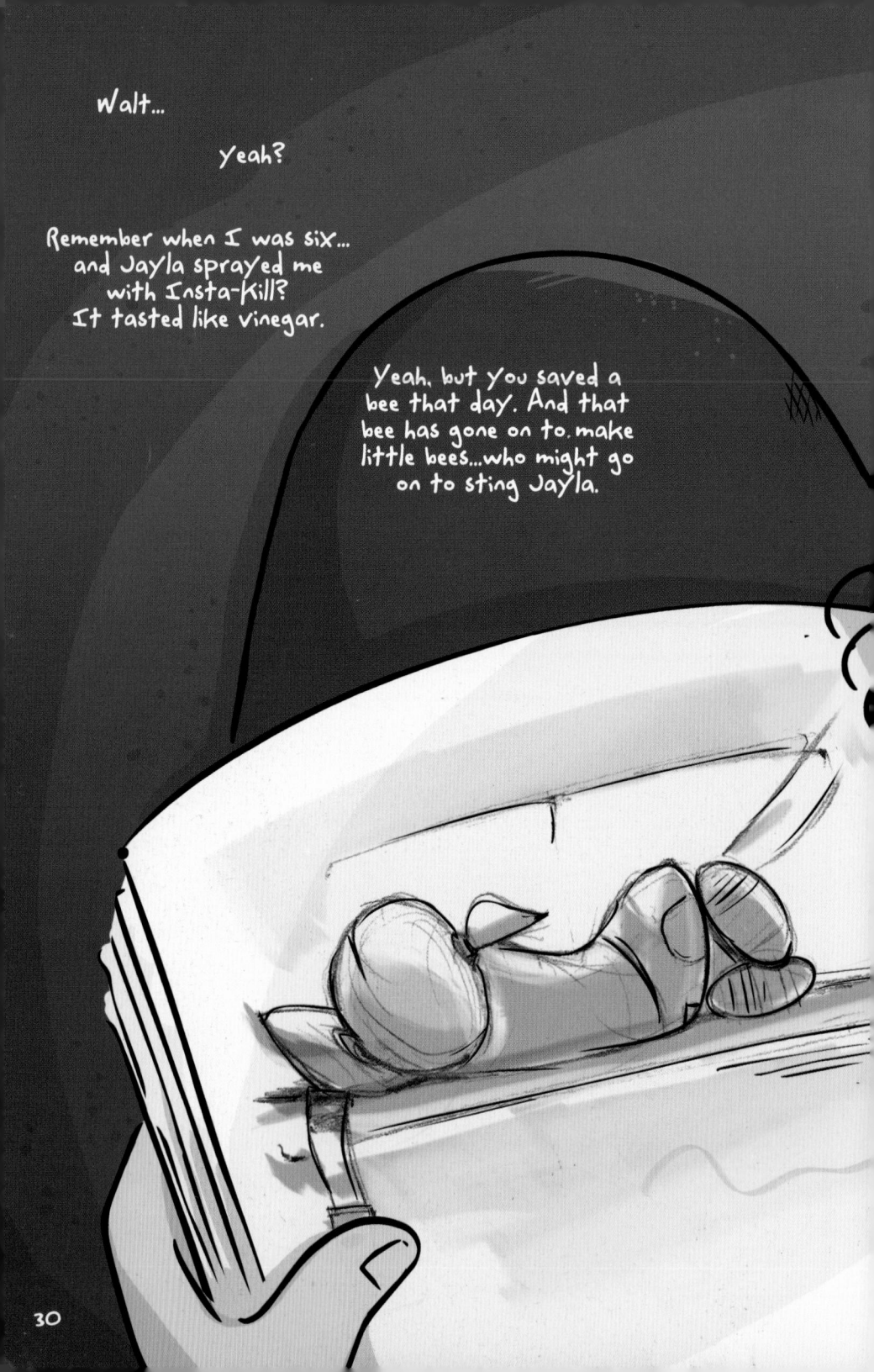
Walt...
Yeah?
Remember when I was six... and Jayla sprayed me with Insta-Kill? It tasted like vinegar.
Yeah, but you saved a bee that day. And that bee has gone on to make little bees...who might go on to sting Jayla.

You think the Insta-Kill made me sick?
No way.

4. A Star Is Bored

Early September...

Do you ever feel like you're living the same day... over... and over... and over?

What do other kids do after school?
Which kids?
Vita, have you made any friends at school?
Well, I met these two guys, Jay and, uh, Jay's friend.

Later That Week...

Limited-edition.

Purple.

Sting Rays!

What does that mean?

Saddle up! We're going to Shoe Town!

SHOETOV
My shoe size is always the first to go!
SALE

Look on the bright side. Now you can afford to buy me lunch!
MR. MUSIC
SALE

I'll never find anything that good again.

Back At Home...
Okay, guess what this is....
TWANG. TWING. TWANG. TWANG. TWANG. TWUNG. TWUNG.
I have no idea.
Here, I'll play it again.
TWANG. TWANG. TWUNG. TWUNG. TWING. TWANG. TWUNG.
That sounded completely different.
Hmm...
Looks like only one of us has an ear for music.

5. What's in a Name?

They're **zebrafish.**

Normal zebrafish have three pigments: **reflective**, **black**, and **yellow**. They're born see-through, but turn opaque as they get older.

But **not** the ones in the fridge. They're **mutants**. They only have the **yellow pigment**. Without the other two, they'll stay transparent **forever**.

So now, I can watch cancer cells BLAH-BLAH-BLAH-size* in real time!

*ME-TAS-TA-size

"Zebrafish!" That's a way better band name!
Where's your Wite-Out? I'm gonna redo my flyer.

6. Reentry

Late September...

Hey, did Mr. Pollack approve my subscription to Green School, Good School?
Your what?
The magazine? Never mind. How are my petitions doing?
I haven't checked lately.
But you posted them, right?
First day of school.
Great! They must be loaded with signatures!
Guaranteed.

Volunteer!
Volunteer!
Please give a hearty "Hej!" to Harald...
Do you support sustainable salmon populations, too?
Whuuut?
Your bracelet!
Salmon is the new orange.

...our foreign-exchange student.

301
SCIENCE
You're in my seat.
That's my seat.
That's my seat.
Take my seat.

7. Upstaged
Finally. Let's go!
I'm gonna stick around. That girl Vita's holding band auditions.
Who's Vita? Is she cute? Should we join?
We don't play anything. I was just gonna stop in to—
I can do a little of this....

Hi. Are you Vita?
I'm Tanya. This is my brother, Walt.

TWANG TWANG TWANG

So, what were you playing?
I was just tuning up.
Locker Jay!

HICCUP!
Hey, Vita!
I guess we can start. I'm Vita. I play guitar. How 'bout you guys?
Plinko!
What's a plinko?
Plinko's his name.
I play Strings of Fury!
Isn't that a video game?
Well, your flyer wasn't specific.

Does anyone play a real instrument?
HEY! How about you?
Nuh-uh.

That Night...

So I'm tuning up. And this girl Tanya says, "I like that song! What's it called?"
Maybe she's into the avant-garde.
Huh?
You know, like, bad on purpose?

I think it's time to go solo.
If you go solo, who's gonna keep you company on the tour bus? Post the flyer again next week. See who shows up!

8. Take Two

One Week Later...

I wrote a song.
I thought maybe your band— when you have a band— could set it to music?
"1,000 Pandas"?
1,000 miles is far to go.
1,000 lawns is a lot to mow.
1,000 pandas left on the map.
1,000 reasons to give a—
Wait...
Is this, like, avant-garde?
What?
Is it supposed to be ba—?
What we think, we become!

How exactly does that work?

Well...if you wrote a song, I could make a video. I'd just need someone to draw us!

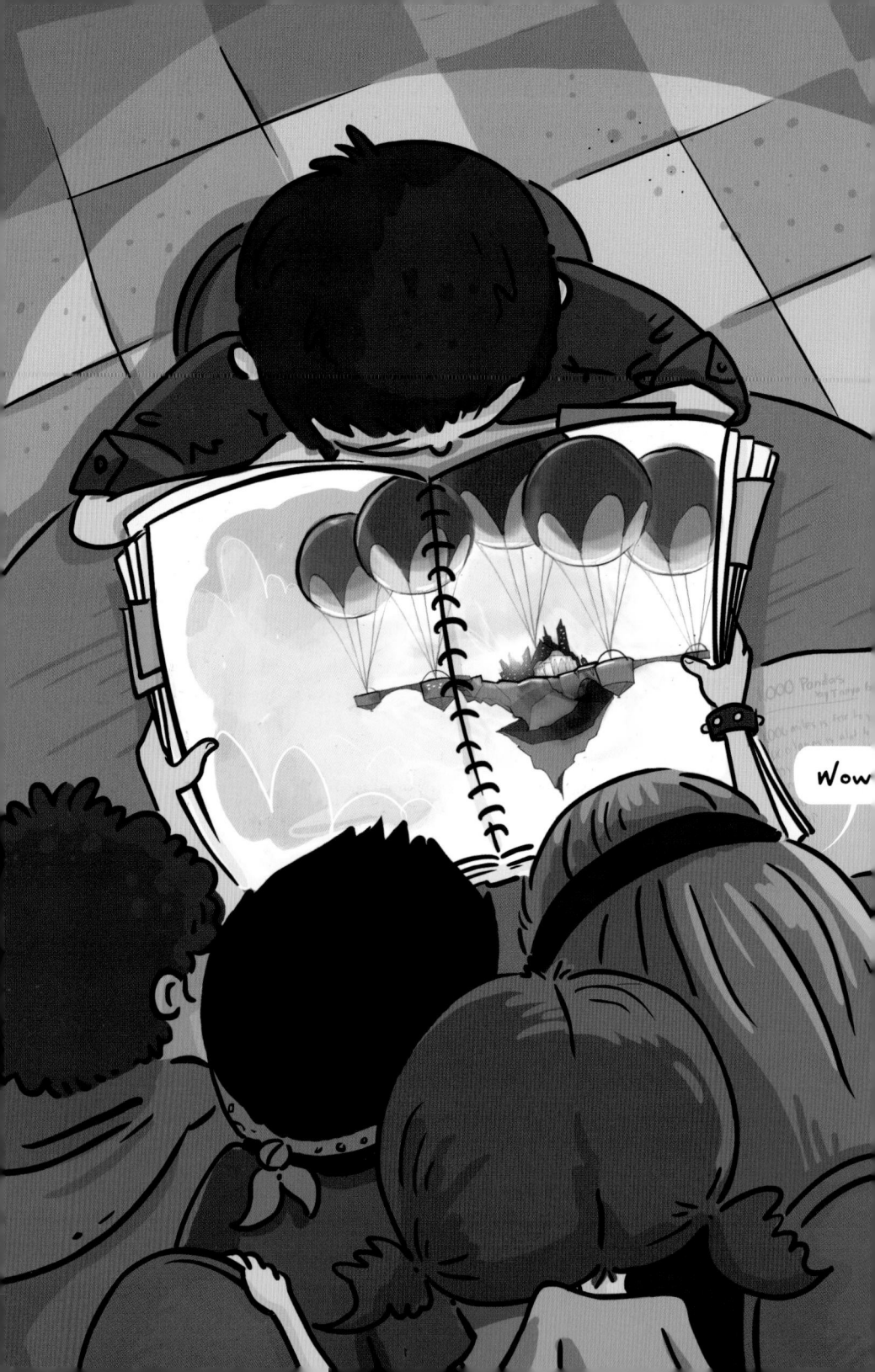
Wow

9. Crushed

Days Later...

Minutes Later...

Later That Week...
Where's Tanya?
At the game.
What for?
She skipped a meeting to watch JV soccer?
Nooo. She skipped a meeting to watch Kyle.
Isn't that the kid with the beard?
I thought that was Gary.
Gary moved on to mutton chops junior year. Kyle stands alone.
Do girls even like facial hair?
I guess Tanya does.
Can we pick up from last week, please? Walt, let's see your sketches for the video.
Huh? Oh right. I'm kind of stumped. Got any ideas?

Can you make me look like this?
You do look like this. It's a photo of you.
Were we supposed to bring a picture?
That's just a headshot. He always carries one.
Okay, so give me a beard. Wait, that's been done. Give me a mustache!

Jay? Vita? Any requests?
Have you seen this jacket? It's got a built-in stereo system with controls on the sleeve and speakers in the hood!
$299.99
I want to wear that in the video.

Walt, can you draw me wearing these?
STING RAYS
Sting Rays? Vita, we're a virtual band. Think big!
Like so!
A bee?

Minutes Later...

04:21
Guest
Home
3
0
STURGEONS
SPIRIT
GO
STURGEONS
7
15

So you'll tell him to change it, right?
Sure. Is later okay? I'm kind of on a date.
GO
STURGEONS!
51
21
8
23

10. One Song

I got a used guitar. My brother thought that I was nuts. But I know who I am...
Uh...
scribble
scribble
The sister of a handsome man.
Pablo! Quit it!
What? I'm just trying to help.
You can't help. Lyrics are very personal.
Don't make 'em too personal. You've got to sing them out loud.

No I don't. We're just making a video. Zebrafish isn't a real band.
That's a real guitar, isn't it? Bands mix live music with video all the time.
Maybe so. But you still can't put on a show with one song.
Who says? The White Stripes once played a single note onstage. Not even a whole song.
TWANG
Like this?
Who'd show up for that?
If it was your show? Me.

11. Intensification

...this kid Tang went to our school. He was such a good singer, nobody knew his last name.
One day Tang agreed to sing Happy Birthday for the principal, a cappella.
So the whole school gathered in the auditorium. There was no spotlight then, so Tang could see everyone staring up at him. Some kids claim they heard "Happy Birthdahhh..."
Where? Where?
ICK!
just before he THREW UP ONSTAGE! Right where you're sitting now!

Ahem....

Sorry.

Now that we're all **here**, I can tell you my idea.

I was thinking we could put on a show. **Here**, in the auditorium.

I'd play guitar while our video played behind me, on the **big screen!**

If you're gonna sing, what's the point of making a video?

Just me singing says recital. Me singing in front of a **twelve-foot** video...?

That's rock and roll!
She's right. The only difference is, the music comes out of her, not the video.
Cool. That's less work to do on the video.
It's a win-win!
doink
A show! Vita, that's brilliant! Now we can sell tickets and make it a real fund-raiser! Like Rock the Rainforest! We should talk to Principal Pompano to reserve a date!
HIC–!
I can help with that!

12. Impact

TANYA BURBOT! Your mother's here to pick you up.

TANYA BURBOT! Your mother's waiting.

I wonder where she goes.

After School...

Vita! What are you doing here?
My brother works upstairs. So, what? You volunteer here now?
You sound mad.
If you were gonna quit Zebrafish, you should've said so. Instead of just bein' a no-show!
I have to be here.
Have to?
Listen. I didn't say anything before, because I don't want people to get weird around me. But weird is better than mad.
So...
I have leukemia. Being sick is a major time suck.
beep *beep*
That's my mom. I've gotta go. I'll try to be at the next meeting, okay?

HOSPITAL ENTRANCE

What's with you?

Leukemia's cancer, right?

Yeah. Why?

Is it a bad one?

It's usually treatable. But patients have to go through a lot of chemo. Sometimes for up to two years.

Chemo didn't work for Mom.

Well...chemo's not a cure. It just kills cancer cells. The problem is, the cells can spread. With Mom's kind of cancer, the cells spread faster than the chemo could kill them.

sigh

C'mon, Vita. Let's take a walk.

gasp

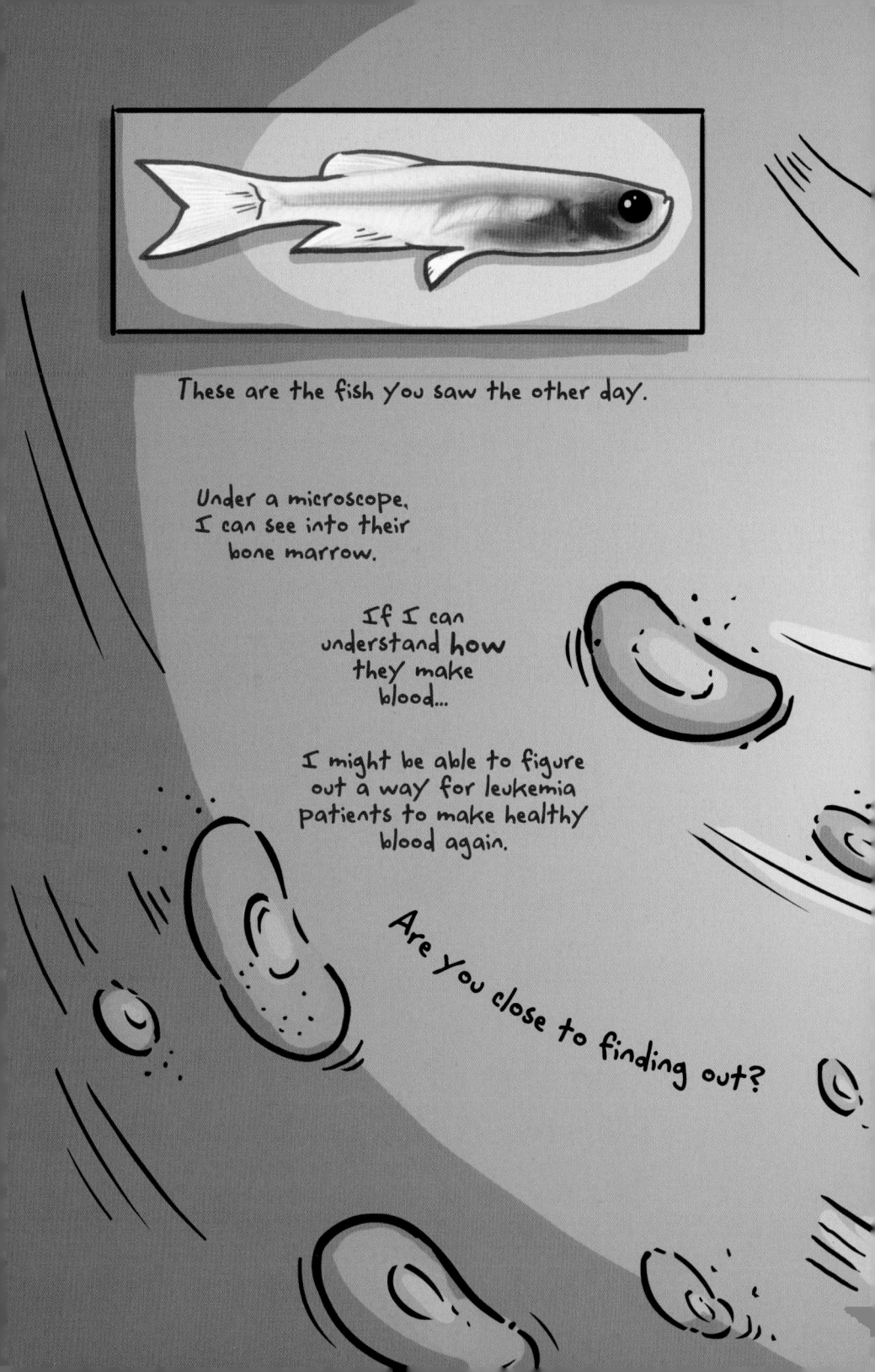
These are the fish you saw the other day.
Under a microscope, I can see into their bone marrow.
If I can understand how they make blood...
I might be able to figure out a way for leukemia patients to make healthy blood again.
Are you close to finding out?

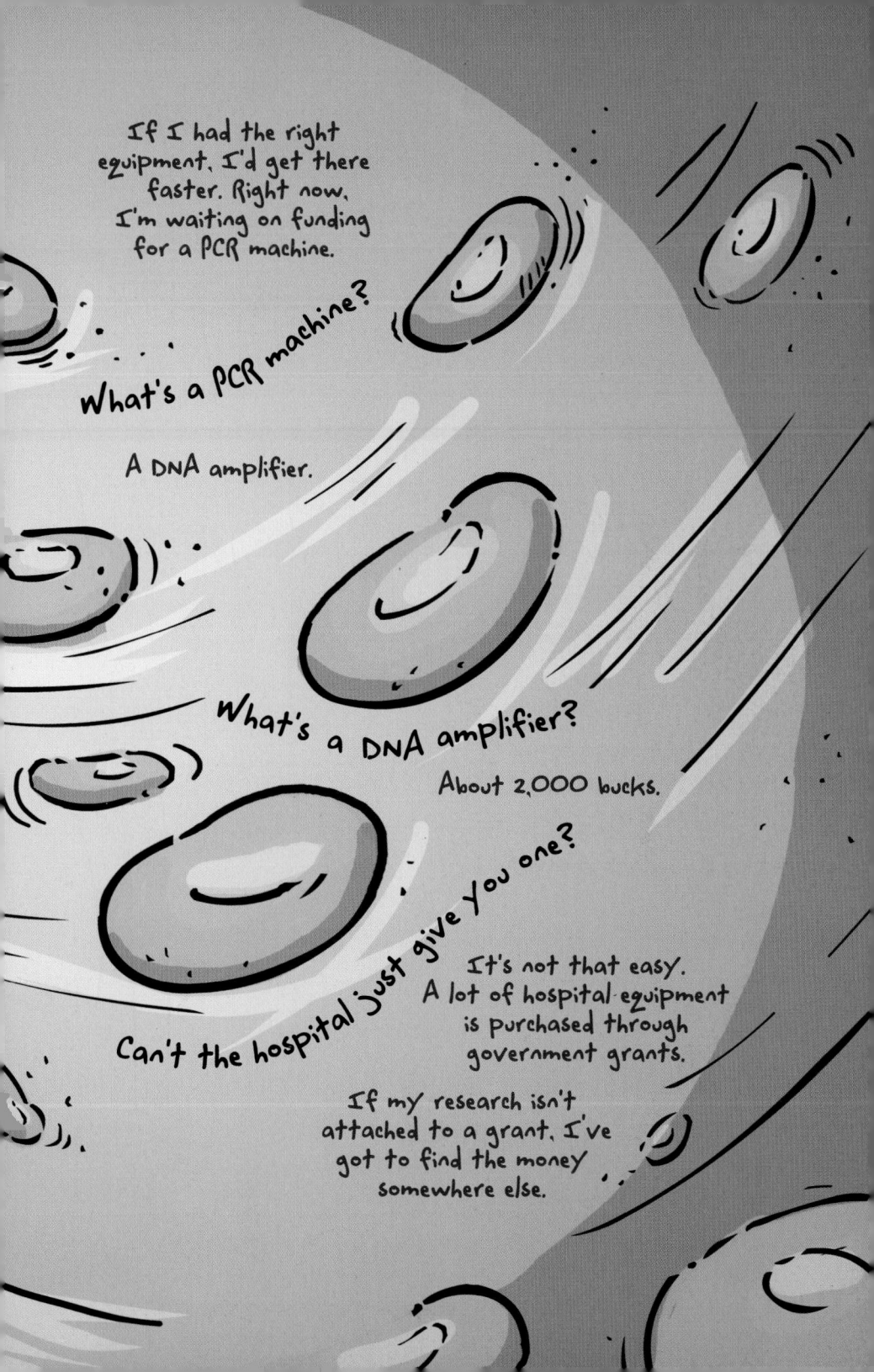
If I had the right equipment, I'd get there faster. Right now, I'm waiting on funding for a PCR machine.
What's a PCR machine?
A DNA amplifier.
What's a DNA amplifier?
About 2,000 bucks.
Can't the hospital just give you one?
It's not that easy. A lot of hospital equipment is purchased through government grants.
If my research isn't attached to a grant, I've got to find the money somewhere else.

13. Intervention

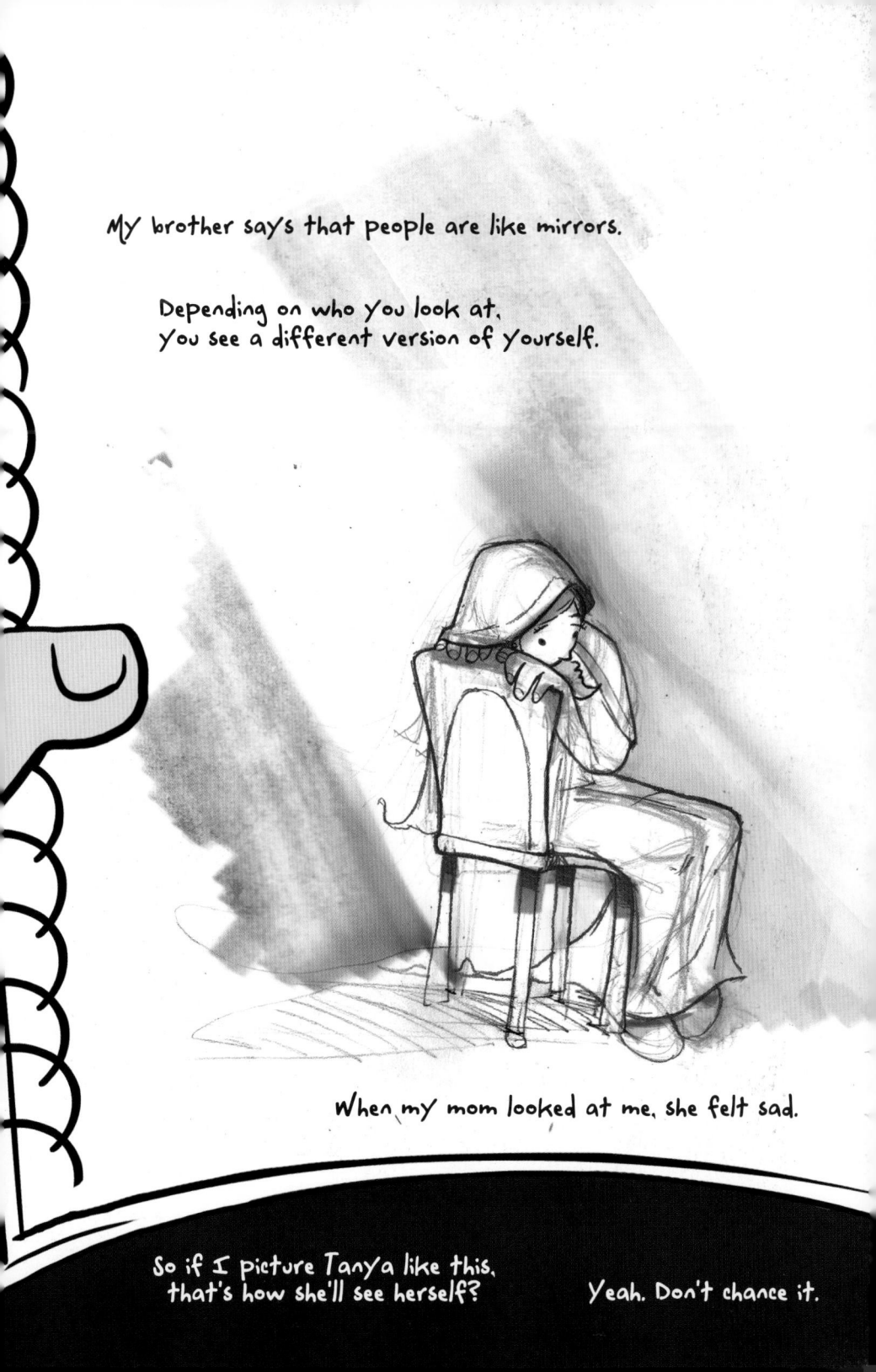
My brother says that people are like mirrors.
Depending on who you look at, you see a different version of yourself.
When my mom looked at me, she felt sad.
So if I picture Tanya like this, that's how she'll see herself?
Yeah. Don't chance it.

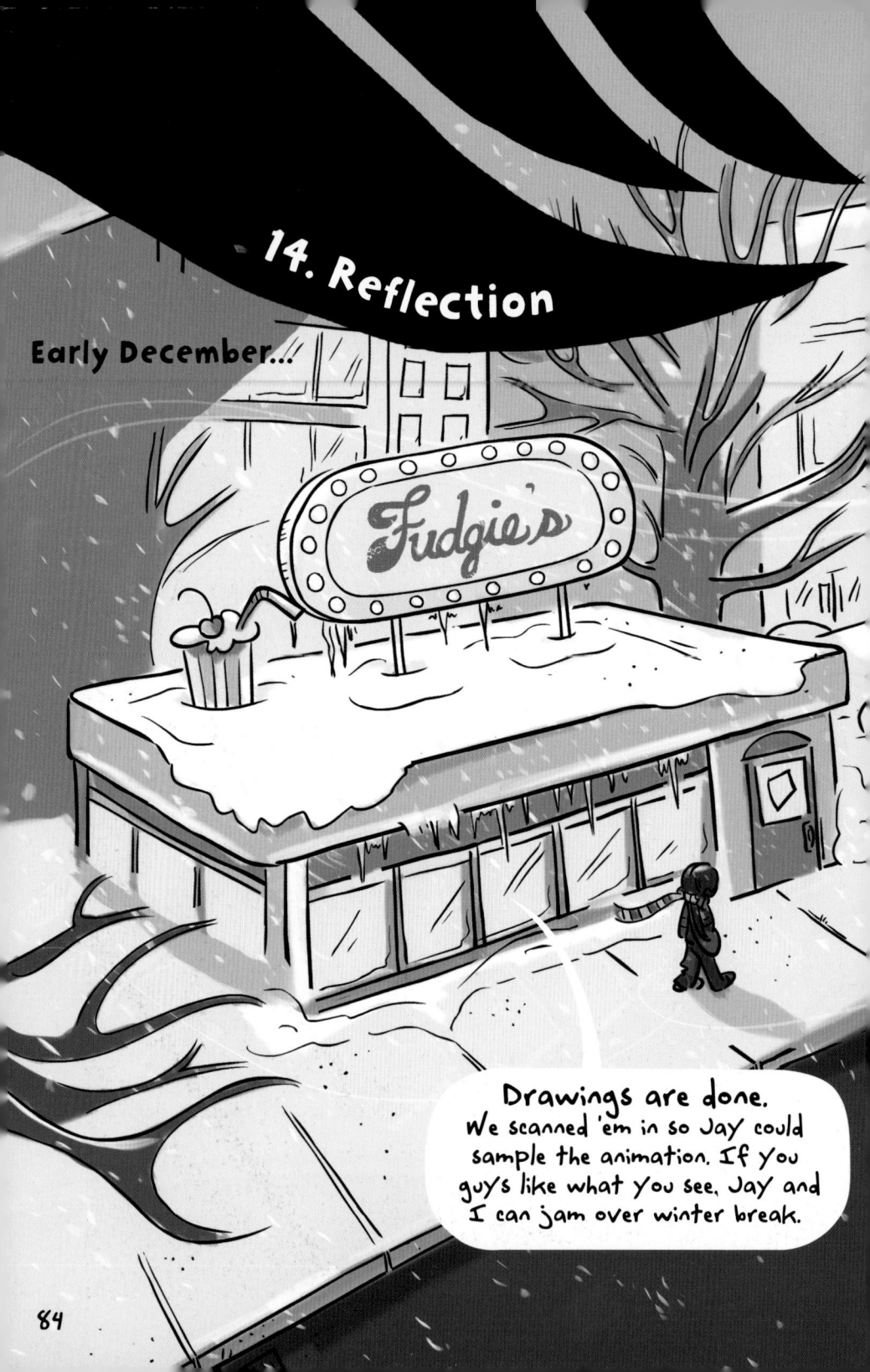
14. Reflection
Early December...
Fudgie's
Drawings are done.
We scanned 'em in so Jay could sample the animation. If you guys like what you see, Jay and I can jam over winter break.

Vita, you changed the words. I like it.
Let me hear next!

Hey, it's me! As a **wizard**?
HICCUP!
Think of it like comfort wear for the traveling activist.
You're here!

CLICK
Here's Jay in his amazing techno-dreamcoat.
Jay.jpg
He looks so old!
Hey, Jay, that's what you'll look like as a senior!
CLICK

And here's Plinko.
Domo arigato, Mr. Mustachio.
...as Hercule Poirot!
Plinkerton.jpg
Me next?
The wrestler?
Best for last!

CLICK
I'm still a bee.
No, I made you a queen bee!
It's the same thing!
I think it's perfect.
Nuh-uh. Queen bees have huge bellies—three times bigger than the average bee!
Bees are tiny creatures, but they do amazing things. Totally out of proportion to their size. They spread pollen to make food! They sustain life!

Vita, check this out....
I can fly. That's a plus.

Fame is a bee.
It has a song—
It has a sting—
Ah, too, it has a wing.
Er-what?
We had to memorize a poem last year. That's the shortest one he could find.
I happen to like Emily Dickinson.
Vita's gonna be famous.
She has a song, she has a sting... and now, she's got wings.

15. Jam Session
Winter Break...
You better cross your fingers, you'll never feel my stinger. I'm a queen bee....

Across Town...

January. Back in School...

How does he expect us to sell 2,000 tickets?

16. Make It Better

February...

I hope we're not playing dodgeball again. When are we going to do something useful in gym? Like...

Here you guys are!
grab
plunk
Wanna help hang posters?
Can't. We've got gym.
Let's meet up after.
Sweet. I'll hunt down tape.

READY!
AIM!
SPTOOOOOOOOOOOOOOOOOOOT!
OOF!
EEP!
ACK!
GET HELP!

What happened? I heard you broke your back in three places and there was blood everywhere.
I don't understand. You used your inhaler right before class!
I sort of forgot.
Forgot? Oh no! I distracted you with my JU-JIT-SU! I've broken the code of Bushido!

Could ya make it up to Buh—uh... Shish-kebab by hanging up posters? Check it out....
We're using the power of rock to make it better.
unroll
ZEBRAFISH!
MAKE IT BETTER
SHOW ON FRIDAY!!
Making it better is the third virtue of Bushido...!
gasp
It's a sign!
I know. I've got 20 of them! Let's shake a leg!

17. Preshow

March...

A fish?
He's a zebrafish.
Our band's namesake! I thought it'd be stripe-ier.
Let's call him Panda. He can be the mascot for our fund-raiser.
What do pandas have to do with it?

We're raising money for pandas.
No we're not. We're getting a PCR machine!
What?
What! It's better than handing over a plain old check. This shows that we put thought into it.
Wait, who's this machine for?
The hospital. To study diseases like...you know, leukemia.

This was your idea?
Well, I know you. I don't know any pandas.

18. Zebrafish Effect

April...

Where's the cord to your amp?
Chimp ate it. It's working off of batteries now.
ZEBRAFISH!
MAKE IT BETTER
CONCERT TONIGHT

So let's give it up for peace, love, and Zebrafish!
SHHH
SHHH
SHHH

SHHH

I got a used guitar.
My brother thought that I was nuts.

But I know who I am:
An indy girl with a purple mutt.
DANGER
HIGH VOLTAGE
DO NOT TOUCH!
MAIN POWER CONTROL

BLARP!
My head was in—Uh-oh.

What the—
?
The curse of TANG!
Stay calm, everyone! AHH! Something touched my foot!
My retainer! Nobody move!

Vita! Keep going!
click
KEEP GOING!
My head was in the clouds
All day long at school—
Suddenly tugged down
By friends who want to change the rules.

Stick to it!
Success don't happen quick.
Stick to it!
Shake it up! Give life a
KICK!

ZEBRAFISH
I'm an indy girl with a—
ZEBRAFISH!
MAKE IT BETTER
Pablo, quit it.
Gwen Greenling. Yearbook staff.
I'd like an exclusive.
FLASH

Zebrafish are (R to L): Vita, Walt, Jay, Plinko, and Tanya.

ZEBRAFISH Unplugged!

A Gwen Greenling Exclusive!

Zebrafish turns a showstopper into a chart topper.

Who let the dog out? *Woof! Woof!*

Local band Zebrafish donates money to the children's research hospital to fund the purchase of a PCR machine. Dr. Pablo Escolar explains, "A PCR machine amplifies DNA. That can help us diagnose diseases like leukemia."

Zebrafish! Behind the Scenes!!!

GWEN: *How long did it take to make the Zebrafish video?*

WALT: Roughly 100 cans of Boost cola.

JAY: Each.

GWEN: *Are you bummed that the video never saw the light of day?*

WALT: That was wrecked!

JAY: I almost Tang'ed on the spot.

WALT: That's gross, man.

JAY: Then 3 days later, it hit me. Let's get it online!

WALT: And 3 days after that, we launched zebrafish.com.

JAY: We've already got hits in the triple digits.

Vita,
The World knows you Rock,
'cause you Rocked the WORLD.
xo—
Jay

THE PLINKOS
260
scratch
You really think so?
Let's ask Mr. Mustachio.
YEARBOOK
DING-DOOONG!

19. Encore

Does it get any easier?
It's not as scary.
4
You think she'll like it?
Let's play it again.

Two!
Three!
Four!
1,000 miles is far to go.
1,000 lawns is a lot to mow.
1,000 pandas left on the map.
1,000 reasons to give a—

START HERE

Many of my books end with the words: "The Beginning" because the end of a story can actually be the start of something **BIG.** So in this space, where **most** books have those words "**THE END**", I wanted to let you know that in this book, on this page, you've hit the spot where things really start. This is where you get invited to get onboard.

Change happens in **2** ways – to you or by you. You can wait around for other people – adults, politicians, college students – to make the **world a better place** or you – **YES, YOU** – can decide to **DO SOMETHING**. Tackle something small or something **HUGE**. Here's a tip: No matter how big the idea, you can start small. Like naming your project – designing a logo – telling a friend. So... find a cause you care about – there are plenty of problems in our world.

Pick a challenge – any challenge...

Safety, health, environment, equal rights, peace....

Think Local – or Global.

Then do something about it.

Write a song, create your own story, throw a fund-raiser.

Create an animated **PSA** (Public Service Announcement).

Build a website. Start a movement!

Think about it – school teaches us to **READ, WRITE, & PROBLEM SOLVE**. Big deal. So what? What are you going to **DO** with those skills? How are you going to use your talents to change the world? Check out www.generationcures.com to see how other kids are

Making a Difference!

Onward,

Peter H. Reynolds

Author / Illustrator / Founder of FABLEVISION (the team that helped create ZebraFish!)

MISSING:
MY RETAINER
SELF ESTEEM
WORKSHOP
"You can do it"
DUFFY MOON
GYM 10 AM
FableVision STUDIOS
BOSTON, MA
Timmy + Hannah 4eva
ZEBRAFISH
BAND AUDITIONS TODAY!!!!
ZEBRAFISH .COM
DOWNLOAD VITA'S SONG "MAKE IT BETTER"
High Score: KATIEBIRD!
3:15
DO YOU PLAY DRUMS? GUITAR? PAN FLUTE? ANYTHING?
DO YOU LIKE TO ROCK!?
with Vita
THANK YOU Z-TEAM!!
Auditions!!! SCHOOL PLAY "CADUCE
Based on the Caledonian Chronicle
AUDITORIU
Zebrafish TONIGHT!
Retainer found! call Gwen 555-2248
SCHOOL
ELECTIO
Save the Planet.

Did you LOVE this book?

Want to get access to great books for FREE?

Join

Simon & Schuster IN THE bookloop

where you can

Read great books for FREE!

Get exclusive excerpts

Chat with your friends

Vote on polls

Log on to everloop.com

and join the book loop group!